Acting Edition

Fade

by Tanya Saracho

∥SAMUEL FRENCH∥

FOR PRODUCTION INQUIRIES

UNITED STATES AND CANADA
info@concordtheatricals.com
1-866-979-0447

UNITED KINGDOM AND EUROPE
licensing@concordtheatricals.co.uk
020-7054-7298

Each title is subject to availability from Concord Theatricals Corp., depending upon country of performance. Please be aware that *FADE* may not be licensed by Concord Theatricals Corp. in your territory. Professional and amateur producers should contact the nearest Concord Theatricals Corp. office or licensing partner to verify availability.

This work is published by Samuel French, an imprint of Concord Theatricals Corp.

<TITLE> was first produced by the Name of producer, production company in place on date. The performance was directed by director, with sets by set designer, costumes by costume designer, etc, etc. The Production Stage Manager was stage manager. The cast was as follows:

ROLE . . . . .Actor

ROLE . . . . .Actor

ROLE . . . . .Actor

ROLE . . . . .Actor

ROLE . . . . .Actor

FADE was first produced at the Denver Center for the Performing Arts (Artistic Director, Kent Thompson) in Denver, Colorado on February 5, 2016. The performance was directed by Jerry Ruiz, with sets by Timothy R. Mackabee, costumes by Meghan Anderson Doyle, lights by Richard Devin, and sound by Tyler Nelson. The Stage Manager was Randall K. Lum. The cast was as follows:

LUCIA .... Mariana Fernandez
ABEL .... Eddie Martinez

FADE was produced at Primary Stages in New York City on January 25, 2017. The performance was directed by Jerry Ruiz, with sets by Mariana Sanchez, costumes by Carisa Kelly, lights by Amith Chandrashaker, sound by M.L. Dogg, and casting by Stephanie Klapper Casting. The Stage Manager was Alfredo Macias. The cast was as follows:

LUCIA .... Annie Dow
ABEL .... Eddie Martinez

CHARACTERS

LUCIA – Late twenties, Mexican-born, acculturated. When in Mexico one would call her a "fresa," but here, she's just an Americanized Mexican who navigates the code-switching between Spanish and English as well as the rest of her (globalized) generation. (This is the "Tuitear" and "Googolear" generation.)

ABEL – Early thirties, born in the U.S., Mexican-American but quite Mexicanized. Born and raised in LA, proud of his Mexican heritage. Got a little bit of a chip on his shoulder. Oh, by the way, don't ask about his tattoos because it really bothers him to talk about them, okay? Just don't. He gets grumpy.

SETTING

An office in a film studio. One of those generic itinerant writer's offices in the writers' building where coat after coat of paint covers up years of nail holes and career disappointment. The place has seen decades of bad writing, receding hairlines, and frantic all-night writing sessions.

TIME

Like, now. And all scenes take place after work hours.

AUTHOR'S NOTES

(/) denotes an overlap. The following line of dialogue is meant to start when an (/) appears in the text. The overlapping is very important. It just sounds like people do when they normally interrupt each other. It's not necessarily trying to talk over one another – although sometimes it is.

A note about the translations:
The Spanish is translated at the top of the script, but after a while I stopped translating. By then, you're into this Spanglish/Espangles world and context clues should carry you through.

Scene One

(Night.)

(A generic studio office. The sound of a faraway vacuum cleaner can be heard.)

*(**LUCIA** appears in the open door frame, holding a box of personal effects. The light, outlining her in shadow. She stands still at the threshold, taking in the moment because, well, she's having all the feels as she stands there. Finally, she takes a step forward and finds the light. It's real office-bright in there. Not kind on the pores. That's not going to work. She puts down the box, explores the office. Looks around. Looks out the big window and ends up by her desk. She tries out her office chair... Goldilocks moment: it's too tall. She adjusts. Zoom. The drop startles her. Now it's too short. She fiddles with it until she gets it juuust right. While she's still messing with it, **ABEL**, the janitor, enters to take out the trash.)*

*(**ABEL** sneaks back out. After a moment, we hear the vacuum cleaner in the distance. **LUCIA** takes in her new domain.)*

(Fuck it. She's here. Might as well make the best of it. She starts unpacking the box, putting knick-knacks on a shelving unit: a Machete figurine still in the box, a Catrina doll, a picture of her parents – you know, that sort of thing.)

(She then takes out a large, framed poster of a book cover that reads: "The Definitive Guide to Nothing, by Lucia Ballesteros." She stands on the desk and goes to place it on the top shelf when the

7

whole thing comes crashing the fuck down. Shit
goes everywhere.)

LUCIA. Puta madre… *[Motherfucker…]*

(Great, she broke the fucking thing. Now what?
She stands there, over it all. What a fucking day.
She thinks for a moment, then goes to the door and
stands at the threshold to call the janitor.)

Disculpa…disculpa. ¿Joven? ¿Me podrías ayudar por
favorcito? *[Excuse me…excuse me. Young man? Could you*
help me please?]

(She goes into the hallway.)

¿Podrías venir por favor? *[Could you come here please?]*

(The vacuum cleaner shuts off. After a little bit,
LUCIA *enters, followed by* ABEL.*)*

¿Me ayudas a arreglar esto por favorcito? Han de estar
mal atornilladas. Te lo agradecería mil. *[Could you help*
me with this, pretty please? They must be screwed in wrong. I'd
be so grateful.]

(ABEL goes to reset the shelving units as LUCIA
inspects the cracked picture frame and then goes
back to text at her desk as ABEL keeps working on
the shelves.)

(ABEL has finished putting up the two shelves and
starts to head out. As he's about to disappear, and
without looking up from her smartphone:)

Me salvaste la vida. Mil gracias… *[You saved my life.*
Thanks a bunch…]

(ABEL nods and goes. After a few moments we can
hear the vacuum cleaner again.)

Scene Two

*(LUCIA is on the office phone. The writer's
assistant is mansplaining on the other line, and
LUCIA's tone is different than it was with ABEL.
Girlier. Almost ditzy.)*

LUCIA. Yeah, sorry, they're saying I need to watch the whole
season, but I'm not understanding the, yeah, the studio
streaming thing so I can start watching the episodes.
Yeah. I'm typing in the log-in you gave me but... Oh,
right. Okay, let me try that. *(Beat.)* Hey, that worked.
Yeah, I think I'm in. Okay, thank you and sorry I'm so
stupid at computer things. Yeah, thanks again...

*(She types something in and clicks – the episode
comes on.)*

ROSA. *(Voiceover.)* Do you know what's the hardest thing
about being brown and from the barrio, like I am?
It's knowing that I'll never be one of them. Knowing
that all they'll ever see is my brown-brown skin. It's my
curse.

LUCIA. Trágame tierra... *[Kill me...]*

*(LUCIA's hands go to her mouth. Oh, gawd, it's
so bad! She shuts it off and her head goes to her
hands.)*

*(ABEL opens the door. When he notices LUCIA is
at her desk, he knocks to get her attention, which
startles her.)*

¡Ay, me asustaste!

*(She goes back to the computer and clicks on the
episode again. ABEL stands there for a moment. He
then quietly goes to empty the trash from the bin
next to the desk as the clip plays again.)*

ROSA. *(Voiceover.)* Do you know what's the hardest thing
about being brown and from the barrio, like I am?
It's knowing that I'll never be one of them. Knowing

that all they'll ever see is my brown-brown skin. It's my curse...

> (**ABEL** *leaves as* **LUCIA** *keeps laser-focused on the screen. Steeling herself.*)

Scene Three

(**LUCIA** *is on the couch, holding a binder and some pages, crying.* **ABEL** *comes in, earbuds firmly placed in his ears, but when he sees* **LUCIA** *in an obvious emo state, he immediately starts to leave.*)

LUCIA. No, pásale. *[No, come in.]*

(*Taking off his earbuds:*)

ABEL. Huh?

LUCIA. Que le pases. *[I said come in]*

(*She points to the trash can, which is overflowing with balled-up papers. Her eyes still on the script she's been studying, even when she stands.*)

Date vuelo. Es pura mierda. *[Go crazy. It's all shit.]*

(**LUCIA** *reaches at the shelf for a Kleenex when the whole thing comes tumbling down, again. This makes her start bawling again.* **ABEL**'s like, "Great, this bitch is a mess.")

(*Feeling toda sorry for herself:*)

Fuck all my life…

ABEL. Well, those shelves aren't too sturdy. They keep puttin' them up and takin', 'em down, so of course they're gonna be loose.

(**LUCIA**'s head shoots up. A pause. She stares at **ABEL** as if she's looking at him for the first time.)

LUCIA. You speak English.

ABEL. Yup.

(*Pause.*)

LUCIA. So why have I been speaking to you in Spanish?

ABEL. Um, I don't know.

(**ABEL** *starts fixing the shelves.*)

LUCIA. Why did I do that?

ABEL. Couldn't tell you.

(Beat.)

LUCIA. Sorry.

ABEL. 's okay.

LUCIA. You know how sometimes you go on autopilot?

ABEL. No.

LUCIA. Like you know when you assume?

ABEL. I don't assume stuff like that.

LUCIA. Oh. *(Beat.)* I guess I do. Which I didn't even know I did.

(ABEL *starts to go, then* LUCIA, *so fucking needy:*)

People don't like it here right? Like in LA.

ABEL. I don't know.

LUCIA. Yeah. They don't. Mexicans don't like it here. I was at this restaurant the other day – by myself, like a total loser because, well, I know zero people in this town – so my waitress was taking my order and to me it's obvious that Spanish is her first language, right? Her accent was just, well, of a person who'd be more comfortable in Spanish. So she's taking my order and I'm like, "Me puedes traer agua por favor?" and she shoots all this shade and all this attitude – and she refuses to answer me in Spanish. I'm like here thinking, "It's OBVIOUS you speak Spanish. Why are we playing this little game? I'm trying to make it easy for you." Just ridiculous.

ABEL. Sometimes they don't let you speak it at work.

LUCIA. Oh, well, I guess that's / true. But she'd rather struggle with her broken English than answer me in Spanish when it's obviously easier for her?

ABEL. Sorry...but what do you mean it was "obvious"?

LUCIA. What was obvious?

ABEL. You said that you spoke Spanish to her because it was "obvious" that she spoke Spanish. What does that mean?

LUCIA. Like she looked like she spoke Spanish.

ABEL. Like I look.

(**LUCIA** *tries to recover.*)

LUCIA. Like…*we* look.

(**ABEL** *nods in understanding.*)

ABEL. Right.

(*Alright, why did this just get awkward?*)

LUCIA. I'm sorry. (*Beat.*) Me assuming you speak Spanish wasn't like an insult. It was like a good thing. I do it because…I mean, it's actually what I'm most comfortable with. And it's a little like, "We're in this together" when I do it, you know what I mean?

ABEL. We're in what together?

LUCIA. I'm just saying that it's my comfort tongue, so whenever I get a chance to speak it, it's like taking off a tight belt, you know? Like…

(*She makes a sound like she just unbuckled her pants. They just stand there, so fucking awkward.*)

Wait. Are you even Mexican / …? I'm sorry, I totally just assumed…

ABEL. Of course. No, I am. I just try not to speak it at work, you know?

LUCIA. Wait. Why?

ABEL. Why I try not to speak Spanish at work?

LUCIA. Yeah.

ABEL. I don't know. Maybe because this is America?

(*Beat.*)

LUCIA. Are you serious?

ABEL. Yeah. Last I checked.

LUCIA. Alright, Donald J.

ABEL. What?

LUCIA. Nothing.

(*Tense pause.*)

ABEL. You have a good night.

   *(**ABEL** puts on his earbuds and leaves.)*

LUCIA. Whoa.

   *(**LUCIA**'s like, "What just happened?")*

Scene Four

(The room is dark except for the light coming from the computer. LUCIA *is watching the pilot again, on the big desktop. She eats chips and has her feet on the desk as she reacts to the shitty dialogue.)*

JACK. *(Voiceover.)* Who is she?

STAN. *(Voiceover.)* She's a whole lot of trouble, is what she is. Raised in the projects, father killed by the INS, had to raise herself up by her own bootstraps. It wasn't a pretty life.

JACK. *(Voiceover.)* Yeah, but WHO is she?

(The cheesy procedural music rises.)

STAN. *(Voiceover.)* That, you'll never find out, my friend. That's her Latin mystery.

*(*LUCIA *makes a face at that last bit.* ABEL *enters with the vacuum cleaner.)*

ABEL. Oh, I thought you weren't here cuz the lights are –

LUCIA. Oh, yeah no, you can turn on the lights if you need to.

ABEL. No, that's okay. I'll come back – when *you're gone.*

LUCIA. You don't have to…

(He's gone.)

…I'm going to be here a while.

(Why is everything terrible? Ugh.)

Scene Five

(LUCIA's on the couch, reading an outline when ABEL enters.)

LUCIA. Hey.

(ABEL gives her one of those tight, purse-lipped smiles and makes a beeline for the trash. Before he gets a chance to exit, a cheery LUCIA engages him.)

Sorry. Trash is stinky today. I was eating corn nuts.

(She waits for a response. He gives her a half-nod.)

That's all they got upstairs. My boss, he lives on them. *(Beat.)* Isn't that like a heart attack waiting to happen, all that corn? Corn's bad, right?

(Pause.)

In the morning, first thing he eats is what we call "corn nut cereal" which consists of a mouthful of corn nuts chased down by a swig of Diet Coke.

Like over and over, so it's basically like cereal in his stomach. I'm gonna turn into one giant corn nut if I keep eating this shit.

ABEL. You want me to open a window?

LUCIA. No, it's fine. I'm done. See?

(She tosses the bag of corn nuts into the trash. ABEL looks at it and comes to grab the wrapper.)

Oh, you don't have to do that.

ABEL. I'm gonna have to get it sooner or later.

LUCIA. Sorry.

(ABEL goes to leave again, but LUCIA interrupts his exit again.)

What's that tattoo you have there?

ABEL. Just a tattoo.

(He starts to leave with the trash when once again:)

LUCIA. Hey, wait. Hold on. The other day, I'm sorry if I – did I offend you with the whole Spanish thing?

ABEL. I wouldn't say you offended me, no. Not offended.

LUCIA. I, what then?

ABEL. You nothing.

LUCIA. Oh, good then. I just…I wouldn't want to offend you. You're like the only, well, you're the only other… *one of us* I ever see around here so I wouldn't want to, you know…

ABEL. Everyone on the cleaning crew's "one of us," so.

LUCIA. Right. But you're the only one who's talked to me. That's why…well, the whole Spanish thing. Don't you think we sort of have to claim these spaces? We're in Trump's America, we have to be militant about speaking our mother tongue whenever the hell we want –

ABEL. Our "MOTHER tongue"?

LUCIA. You know what I mean.

> *(Beat.)*

Well, I'm just glad I didn't offend, that you weren't offended.

ABEL. Yeah. I wasn't. / You can't help where you're from.

LUCIA. Good. I'm glad.

> *(Beat.)*

Wait. *(Beat.)* What did you say? *(Beat.)* Did you say, "I can't help where I'm from"? What is that supposed to mean?

ABEL. You're Mexican, right?

LUCIA. Yeah.

ABEL. From Mexico. Born there?

LUCIA. Yeah?

ABEL. Raised in a specific kind of way?

LUCIA. What do you mean?

ABEL. The way you talk.

LUCIA. What, like I have an accent?

ABEL. No, I just recognize the way you talk. In Spanish. I waited tables for a while and the kind of Mexicans that would come in, you always knew what kind of table they were going to be, because their little fresita accent.

LUCIA. You're calling me a fresa?

ABEL. Not as an insult. Just what it is.

LUCIA. I'm so not a fresa! I have to have a job, first of all, / my daddy didn't set up some trust fund for me –

ABEL. I'm just saying that you can't help where you're from.

LUCIA. Where I'm from? Where are you from?

ABEL. Here. El Sereno.

LUCIA. Oh. I thought you were Mexican.

ABEL. Yeah, I am. But I was born here. My grandparents are from Guanajuato.

LUCIA. Not even your parents? Your grandparents are the Mexican ones.

ABEL. We're ALL the Mexican ones.

LUCIA. Right, but that makes you more like…Mexican-American.

ABEL. No. I'm a Mexican who happened to be born in El Sereno. Just by accident.

LUCIA. Ah.

        (*Tense-ass pause.*)

ABEL. Does stink like corn nuts in here.

LUCIA. Sorry.

ABEL. You don't have to say sorry / to me.

LUCIA. Hopefully it'll dissipate now that you're taking the trash. Thank you.

        (**ABEL** *starts to go.* **LUCIA***'s like, "Shit, it does stink in here." She goes to see if she can open the window.*)

ABEL. You wanna crank the window?

LUCIA. Yeah, I think / I'm going to open it.

ABEL. It has sort of a…there's a little trick to it. You want me to crank it open for you?

LUCIA. No, I don't need you to "crank" it for me, / thank you.

ABEL. Okay, but they're from the forties when this studio got built so they're a little tricky. / You just gotta crank it.

LUCIA. I got it. Thanks.

ABEL. Well. Give a holler if you need my help.

LUCIA. I'm fine.

> (**ABEL**'s like, "Suit yourself She-Ra," and bounces.
> **LUCIA** starts to hit the pane with her shoulder.
> After a while, **ABEL** comes back.)

ABEL. You sure you don't need help cranking it?

> (**LUCIA** hits the window.)

Te digo que tiene maña.

> (The Spanish makes her stop and look at him.)

LUCIA. Well, look at that. He does speak Spanish after all.

ABEL. Hey, I never said I didn't speak it. I just wasn't gonna answer you with it only cuz you had decided for both of us that we were gonna speak it.

> (Beat.)

You gonna let me crank the window open for you?

LUCIA. Yeah. If you stop saying "crank."

ABEL. Look. It's cuz this is how you open it. You were pushing it and you have to do it like this.

> (Yup. He old-school cranks it.)

LUCIA. Well, now I know. Thank you.

ABEL. You gotta get old school with it.

> (She cracks a smile at "old school," then, lightly:)

LUCIA. Hey. I'm probably going to be here.

> (Pause.)

ABEL. Okay?

LUCIA. Well, if I don't get fired –

ABEL. That's a winning attitude.

LUCIA. No, I'm just saying I want to start from scratch with you.

> *(Extending her hand.)*

Hi, I'm Lucia. Not ever to be pronounced like, "Loo-sha."

ABEL. My hands, they're a little dirty…

> *(She's persistent.)*

LUCIA. And you are…?

> (**ABEL** *finally shakes her hand.*)

ABEL. Abel. Pronounced like Abel. Not like –

LUCIA. Able.

ABEL. Yeah. Who would be named "Able"?

LUCIA. Nobody.

> *(She grabs some Twizzlers from the desk and holds them out.)*

Peace offering, Abel-not-Able?

ABEL. No, thanks. Sorry, but those are nasty. Taste like plastic.

LUCIA. They do, right? All gringo candy does.

ABEL. It sure does.

LUCIA. Sí, ¿verda? Guácala. It's all just fructose and food coloring here. You know what I miss most about Mexico? What I miss most is the good street food. Like the elotes and the jicamas bathed in lime juice and covered in chili powder. Doesn't that make your mouth water?

ABEL. We have that here too.

LUCIA. Oh, it's not even the same. The corn tastes different here.

ABEL. Why do Mexicans always say that?

LUCIA. You know I got actual typhoid from eating on the street?

ABEL. Sorry, you said *typhoid*? Does that even exist anymore?

LUCIA. Of course. Still a Third World country. You just shouldn't eat on the street. Pero con mugrita sabe más rico, ¿apoco no?

> (**ABEL** *is almost charmed by that last comment... almost.*)

When I was a kid, I was totally addicted. I used to bribe my maid with scrungies and bracelets / so she'd sneak me out to –

ABEL. You bribed your "MAID."

LUCIA. With scrungies, because I was so addicted to eating elotes from the street.

ABEL. And you still maintain you're not a fresa?

LUCIA. No, it wasn't like that. Chatita was with us since I was a baby. I loved her so much.

ABEL. Oh, man.

LUCIA. You know everyone in Mexico has a maid, it doesn't make you a fresa.

ABEL. I can assure you my grandparents didn't have a maid.

> (*Suddenly realizing she might be steppin' into it.*)

LUCIA. But...that was the olden days. Now, everyone's got one. Even maids have maids now. *(Beat.)* Anyway, I used to make Chatita walk me down to get an elote in a cup and well...eventually I caught me some typhoid.

ABEL. Oh, man...

Hey, God don't like ugly.

LUCIA. This is true.

> (*A nice pause. Seizing this opportunity:*)

We made a bad impression on my first day, didn't we? So I'm glad we're resetting.

ABEL. I made a bad impression?

LUCIA. Okay, I made a bad impression.

> (*He tosses her a bone and smiles.*)

ABEL. New jobs, they're always weird...scary at first.

LUCIA. Yeah, well this one is particularly scary. I don't really want to be here.

ABEL. Yeah, there are days I don't want to be at work neither.

LUCIA. No, like I don't think I should be doing this job. The first week, I was throwing up every morning in the parking lot, before coming in.

ABEL. Oh, it's like that huh?

LUCIA. Yeah. *(Beat.)* I have zero idea what I'm doing. When I got hired to write for this, I totally thought I'd be, well, writing. But there's been zero writing involved. There's just been sitting and talking. All day, that's what we do – sit and talk. I sit up there, in that writers' room, terrified all day that they're going to call on me and expect me to say something smart and witty to contribute to the conversation – but thank God that doesn't happen much cuz I don't know any of these terms they throw around. And when they laugh, I don't know what's so funny.

ABEL. Whoever hired you hired you for a reason.

LUCIA. Yeah, my boss hired me, but I don't think he remembers. He thinks I'm the assistant because the only time he's ever talked to me is when he asked me to get him something from the kitchen. Literally. Oh, no. Once he asked me to make him copies of a script. So that one hundred percent tells you what he thinks of my abilities as a writer, right?

ABEL. It'll get better, I guess.

LUCIA. Yeah. *(Beat.)* I have this fantasy that I get fired and I get to go back home – and sure, that means I go back to being broke – but at least I get to keep my dignity, right? And on the plus side, that would mean that I wouldn't have to wake up every morning, five times a week, to come to the same soul-sucking place. I'm never going to get used to that part.

ABEL. You never had no job before?

LUCIA. Not like the kind where you go to an office, no.

ABEL. Then how did you…? Oh, you're married.

LUCIA. What? No I'm not married. *(Beat.)* Oh, man. Because that's the only way I'd be able to stay home, if a man kept me? You ARE Mexican after all, huh? / What year is this?

ABEL. Nah, I just meant / that if you didn't…

LUCIA. No, of course I've earned money in my life. I've just never had an office job. / Or like where you have to go in to an office.

ABEL. I never had an office job. But I've always had to show up somewhere. That trips me out that someone's never / had a job.

LUCIA. Nonono. I've been employed but what I used to do before, one didn't have to go to an office. I mean, I had a home office and I worked out of there. But like, in my PJs so it didn't count.

ABEL. Oh, yeah. I know someone like that. My sister's friend, she does medical billing from her house. I don't know, wouldn't that make you go kind of crazy? I would go stir crazy.

LUCIA. Are you kidding? It was the best. I'm from Chicago and it gets so freakin' cold. You don't ever want to leave the house which makes it perfect for freelancing, because you don't have to go anywhere.

ABEL. Yeah, I heard Chicago's real cold.

LUCIA. "Cold" is not even the word. *(Beat.)* Oh, man. Stop, you're making me homesick.

ABEL. Thinking about the cold makes you homesick?

LUCIA. Yes. The sun and all those palm trees here put me in such a bad mood.

ABEL. I've never heard of the sun putting someone in a bad mood.

LUCIA. Well, you heard it here. Fuck all this sunshine.

> *(They smile.)*

ABEL. Maybe you just need to give it some time.

LUCIA. Maybe. It's just night and day. This is television. I'm a novelist. Okay, I wrote *A* novel. I've written one novel. Mostly, I consider myself that kind of writer. Not like the kind that writes dialogue and camera angles and stuff like that.

ABEL. Wow. You don't seem like someone who'd write a novel, to me.

LUCIA. I don't?

ABEL. No disrespect.

LUCIA. None taken. I think.

    (Wait a minute…)

Wait, what do you mean?

ABEL. I don't know. Like how you are, like how you talk.

LUCIA. Oh. Gotchu. Like I don't sound smart enough / to have written a book. Because novelists, they have to sound a certain way to you.

ABEL. No, you're takin' it the wrong way. For real, I meant no disrespect.

    (Annoyed little beat.)

LUCIA. For your information, the way I talk is the reason my novel did so well. / So.

ABEL. Again, no disrespect.

LUCIA. But you're also not the first to say that I don't sound like someone who'd write a novel. / Probably because I don't write novels. Not in the plural sense. I'm supposed to be writing the second one. Like the one everyone's waiting for, but they've been waiting for almost three years now, so who knows if it's going to come. So now I'm the fucking hag that came to write for TV with absolutely no TV writing experience, which is still surreal to me. Now, I know very well why they wanted me. It's very much because I am Mexican. I don't like fool myself about that.

ABEL. See, now I feel bad. It didn't come out how I wanted…

Well, that would be a first. Mostly I know people who don't get jobs because they ARE Mexican.

LUCIA. Really? Still? *(Beat.)* No, I know very well why I'm here. Trust me. They won't let me forget it. On the first day, one of the other writers – this guy named Gary who's basically a prevention ad for skin cancer with his fake orange tan – he like corrals me in the kitchen, puts his face real close to mine and whispers all gross, "You do know you're the *diversity hire*, right?" And I'm like, "What's that?" He says, "You're only here because you're a Hispanic. It's great, you don't have to try too hard, you're only here to meet the quota."

ABEL. What, like the affirmative action thing?

LUCIA. Yup. And they're just not going to let me forget that that's what I am.

ABEL. Who's not going to let you forget?

LUCIA. Just everyone in the room – the dudes I work with. Little things they say. It's how they treat me. They call me "Mommasita," / which really annoys the crap out of me: "Mommasita." One calles me Sofia Vergara. Ugh. He can't even say "Vergara" right.

ABEL. Ooh. Rough.

People are assholes on this lot. Especially those guys upstairs, like the ones in the bigger offices up there, they always think I'm deaf or something. Like they'll ask me for something but they'll talk real slow and loud – like if I'm simple. / I'm like, motherfucker…

LUCIA. No, don't tell me that. Don't. Oh, God. I hate this place so much.

(A text comes through on ABEL's phone.)

I know I should be grateful. I should just put my head down and stop complaining. I should just shut up and cash that paycheck, / which is the only reason I'm here.

ABEL. Pay that rent.

LUCIA. Yeah. But I'm not here to make a career of this. God, I would shoot myself if this actually became what

I did. Because that takes a certain level of selling out, you know? Those are not real writers up there. They're "Yes Guys." They just say "Yes" all day long.

ABEL. Oh, I know "Yes Guys."

LUCIA. Yeah, well, I'm not wired like that. I just want to get good enough at this to pay off my debt y ya. Back to Chicago I go.

ABEL. I hear ya. Still good they gave you the job.

LUCIA. Well, they had to, for the quota, right? I think the network forces the show to get a token – but fuck it. I'm here. You know, one of the reasons I said yes to the job is because we're nowhere. Like on TV, I mean. You got these white guys writing the most tone-deaf, stereotypical shit. That's why the shit you watch on television is so –

ABEL. Whack? Yeah. I'm not a fan.

LUCIA. Of course you're not. Why would you be? And if they want you for a fan, they better start acting right and fix shit. And I guess that's what they're trying to do now. Like with this show. It has this main character, she's Hispanic / which is...

ABEL. You mean Latina?

LUCIA. What?

ABEL. She's Latina. Not Hispanic.

LUCIA. Whatever.

ABEL. No. Not whatever.

LUCIA. Listen, I'm not going to go get into the whole Latino vs. Hispanic thing with you because if all those think tanks haven't figured out which term we should be using, there's no way you and I are figuring it out. *(Quick beat.)* If you want to get technical, the term is now "Latinx" –

ABEL. It's what?

LUCIA. Yeah, but let's not even – that's a whole other can of worms. So for our purposes, fine, she's *Latina*, okay?

ABEL. What kind?

LUCIA. What kind? Like "What flavor of Latina?"

ABEL. Where is she from?

LUCIA. Well, Abel-not-able, I don't actually know / because strangely enough they won't fucking decide.

ABEL. How do you not know? She has to be a certain kind. Who won't decide?

LUCIA. They won't – the writers upstairs. She HAS to be from somewhere. You can't just be from the Planet Latinia! / But the room won't decide. They refuse to put any thought to it because to them, it doesn't matter. She's just a generic Latina. That's enough for them.

ABEL. Stupid…

You should say something.

LUCIA. I know. I'm trying. I'm working my way up to it, okay? *(Beat.)* She's not *that* bad. In the first season, at least they made her a badass, so that's good. But we do have to work on the rest of it.

I'm goint to try to make her into something that doesn't make you cringe. I mean that's why they brought me in, right? To make it all more authentic.

ABEL. Damn, the show might be in trouble then.

LUCIA. Qué malo.

> *(Not gonna lie. They're kind of enjoying each other a little bit. A beat.)*

ABEL. Alright. I don't want to join you in the unemployment line, here chit-chatting all night long. I better jet.

LUCIA. Ok, Abel-not-like-able. I'll be here.

ABEL. Ta bueno.

> *(He exits. LUCIA's like, "Well that wasn't so bad.")*

Scene Six

*(LUCIA enters, fucking fuming. ABEL follows,
holding one of those big industrial brooms.)*

ABEL. Ey, whatsumatter with you? You look like that Darth
Vader song should be playing as you storm down the
hall.

LUCIA. Aaaggrr!

(She's having a fit.)

I'm going to throw something out the fucking window
right now. Aaaggrr.

ABEL. I vote maybe no? Cuz I really don't feel like going
down there / and cleaning up after you...

LUCIA. Cierra la puerta. Ciérrala, por favor.

(ABEL does so.)

ABEL. Are you okei?

*(LUCIA is enchilada. She's a little firecracker right
now.)*

LUCIA. Why do I even fucking try, Abel?

ABEL. Oh, it's one of those rants.

LUCIA. I'm going to tell you something, Abel. Don't drink
the Kool-Aid. We are knee-deep in the shit-soup that
is Trump's America. All the progress we made with
Obama? Put it out of your head. Rewind and delete, my
friend. You and I are still the fucking Taco Bell dog to
these people, we're little Speedy Gonzales mice at their
feet and, and...it's all the fucking pussy you can grab!

ABEL. I'm a little worried you might have a stroke right
now.

LUCIA. Oh, God, what am I doing in this fucking town!

ABEL. Estás toda red. Why don't you sit down for a little
bit –

LUCIA. I should fucking quit.

ABEL. Whoa. Okay, hold up. Let's take a little breath, come
on, breathe with me.

(She does so.)

¿Qué te pasó?

LUCIA. My stupid boss. *(Beat.)* I turned in my first thing today to him – he just asked us to write down pitches, just ideas for him. It's not like the biggest deal / but it's the first thing I was turning in, so…no, I can't sit right now.

ABEL. Come on, sit down.

LUCIA. It's the first thing I've turned in so of course I'm on edge. And my, my boss comes out of his office before lunch, holding my document in his hands, and says, "Lusha, / could I see you after we wrap up?" I seriously think I flat-lined for maybe three seconds there…

ABEL. Man, can't he get your name right?

LUCIA. I KNOW!

ABEL. What is so hard about Lucia?

LUCIA. Yeah, but he's never looked in my direction, much less said my name. So end of day, we get done, and I sort of stay in the writers' room shooting the shit with the assistant, just waiting until he finally peeks his head in and he's like – "Lucia, could I see you a moment?" So I go into his office –

ABEL. *(Like a heart beat.)* tunTUN.tunTUN.tunTUN.

LUCIA. Basically.

ABEL. And then he yells at you.

LUCIA. Um. No. And then he says, "I'm a man who likes the simple things."

ABEL. Oh, shit.

LUCIA. No, wait. *(Beat.)* He tells me that in the mornings he likes to come out of his bedroom and have his papers fanned out outside of his room, a cup of coffee waiting for him in the upstairs kitchen.

ABEL. He has an upstairs kitchen?

LUCIA. Oh, yes, apparently his house is like four stories with a huge basement that has like a basketball court and a movie theater – it's insane.

ABEL. Man. These fucking people.

LUCIA. I know. But listen to this, apparently he likes his *Variety* and his *Hollywood Reporter* and *Wall Street Journal* and whatever else fanned out in a certain kind of order and his maid, Carmen, hasn't been doing it the proper way. Or she's inconsistent about it. And he's been very clear about this request. And it makes him very angry – in fact, it ruins the rest of his day to know that he is being ignored. "I feel as if she's mocking me," he says.

ABEL. ¿Eso dijo?

LUCIA. Yeah. He literally thinks he's being mocked if you don't organize the papers and fan them out exactly how he wants. Apparently Carmen failed to even have any of the papers there at all this morning and the man blew his lid. Something big went down. He almost fired Carmen or something.

ABEL. These fucking people, man.

LUCIA. But his wife was like, "No, John! She's the best maid we've ever had. She does windows without me having to ask her. / Please work this out with her." Like in tears and everything.

ABEL. Pinches gringos…

LUCIA. And John, my boss, is magnanimous, right? He is just and fair and tells his wife, "Well, if you can get her to understand that she has to fan out the periodicals / exactly as I indicate, then she can stay."

ABEL. Periodicals. Shut up "periodicals."

LUCIA. But then the wife, who apparently has like a condition, bursts into even more tears and says, "But she doesn't speak English, John. How will I ever do that?!" And my boss is like, "Must I solve everything?!"

ABEL. The burden of the White man.

LUCIA. Abel. THIS is why I'm sitting in his office.

    (**ABEL** *doesn't get it.*)

He wants me to call Carmen and explain to her about the magazines.

ABEL. What?

LUCIA. He asks, "Could you communicate in her language that I must have the coffee ready to go by the time I wake up and the magazines pre-arranged to the right of my door? I would really appreciate this."

ABEL. Or Carmen gets fired.

LUCIA. Can you believe it?

ABEL. Oh, yeah. I can believe it. I can believe poor Carmen's going to walk on glass every time the guy's around until she gets a condition herself, man. / But what can she do? Complain to somebody? No, she gotta take it, cuz she probably has three kids at home and they need shoes and uniforms and money for band. So yeah, I can believe that. I can believe your boss is a fucking asshole who should be punched in the face.

LUCIA. No. I mean, can you believe that this is why he brought me in there? Abel, can you believe this guy just... No. Abel...

   Abel! THIS IS WHY HE BROUGHT ME IN THERE. That's all I am to him. To those men up there. I'm just the fucking –

ABEL. Spic?

LUCIA. What?

   (Quick beat.)

   No. Translator. I'm just a translator to him.

ABEL. Oh.

LUCIA. That's all I am to him, Abel.

ABEL. So you called her?

LUCIA. Well, yeah, next I know, without me having said yes, my boss starts dialing his house and he hands me the phone. So what could I do? My first instinct was to be like, "Fuck you, you pig. Is this all you think of me?" But then... What? Was I going to say "No" and leave Carmen hanging? He was about to fire her, and she didn't even know it.

ABEL. Oh, trust me. She knew it. The language of Assholiness is universal.

LUCIA. I'm being serious.

ABEL. Me too. A prick is a prick here or in China, man. What did you say to Carmen?

LUCIA. Well, I tried to speak code. Like, I spoke to her in Spanish, of course, but also, I did it in code. With like a smile the whole time.

ABEL. Like, "Este pinche culero wants you to step up your periodicals game, Carmelita."

LUCIA. Exactly. And then, I get off the phone he thanks me and he immediately goes back to his computer. Like, "I'm done with you and you're of no more use to me." I stand there like an idiot for two seconds and then go. Can you believe that, Abel?

ABEL. What? That your boss is a cabrón?

LUCIA. That my boss only sees me as the translator for his maid and nothing else. To him, that's my value. Because in his mind, I'm on the same level as his maid. We're the same thing.

ABEL. Whatchu mean by that? "You're the same thing"?

LUCIA. Nothing. / Just that –

ABEL. No, I'd like to know just what you mean by that, please. Why would it be so bad if you two were the same thing?

LUCIA. You're not getting it.

ABEL. Okay, then. Explícamelo.

LUCIA. In that room – and no shade to Carmen, but THAT is all my boss will ever see me as. I'll never be his equal in there –

ABEL. Well, no, cuz he's your boss.

LUCIA. No. I'll never be good enough to be seen as one of the writers to him. Because the only exposure he's ever – any of them, actually – have ever had to a Latina is through this kind of exchange. Master and servant.

ABEL. Everything in life is "master and servant." There's only one or the other.

LUCIA. No, Abel...they can't see us in any other context.

ABEL. Right. Only as maids. And janitors.

LUCIA. No, that's not... I didn't mean it like that –

    (Oh, come on, is she going to cry now?)

I was making a statement about the larger... Wait, Abel, don't go, please. Wait.

ABEL. Gotta go be my value and clean some bathrooms.

    (Fuck.)

Scene Seven

(**ABEL** *walks in to change the trash can. On the desk is a box of cookies with a big sign that says: "Peace offering? [Yes, for you, Abel.]" He looks at the box but he doesn't take the cookies. He starts to go. He stops by the door and doubles back to take the box. He takes out a cookie and bites into it. Pretty good. He exits.*)

Scene Eight

       (*ABEL is walking in to place a blue recycling bin next to the trash can when* LUCIA *enters like a dramarama drama queen who's making whatever the fuck she has to share real suspenseful.*)

LUCIA. Abel.

ABEL. Yeah?

       (*Beat.*)

LUCIA. Abel.

ABEL. Yes, that's my name.

       (*Pause.*)

LUCIA. Abel!

ABEL. Lucia!

LUCIA. Abel. I am a dead woman.

       (*Quickly, re: recycling bin.*)

What's that?

ABEL. You're going green.

LUCIA. Finally. *(Beat.)* Abel, did I mention that I am dead.

ABEL. What is happening with you right now? Are you having one of those episodes where you think you're in a telenovela?

LUCIA. Yes. I'm jumping out the window and you can't stop me.

ABEL. You gotta figure out how to open it first.

LUCIA. I don't even know what I just did, Abel. It's like maybe the stupidest thing…or the most brilliant or who knows.

       (*Ding.*)

Wait. Where are you from?

ABEL. El Sereno. I've told you that.

LUCIA. I don't know what kind of place that is. Is that a neighborhood?

ABEL. Yes and no.

LUCIA. What do you mean "Yes and no"?

ABEL. It's LA, everything's a town and a neighborhood.

LUCIA. Yes.

Okay...

Okay...

You are going to help me.

ABEL. You know what...before you drag me down one of your schemes, like when you wanted me to steal that lamp / from five.

(Looking around, proving her point:)

LUCIA. You have to agree that this room is screaming for / an additional lighting source.

ABEL. I'm getting outta here.

LUCIA. Wait, ¡no te vayas! Abelin, I just put my big foot in it y ahora no me puedo rajar. (Beat.) I just promised something that I don't know if I can deliver. Oh, Jesus.

ABEL. You know, a little less suspense would go a long way.

LUCIA. Ay, tú nunca me dejas saborear. Okay, so our protagonist is going to get a love interest. That was like a big note from last season: No one wants to see a lead with no love intrest on TV – single women are sad hags and it's not interesting to the public. Bueno, total – this love interest they came up with was going to be your regular white heartthrob.

ABEL. Of course.

(ABEL's still waiting for the punchline.)

LUCIA. So these assholes were all up there pitching – "He's a detective." "He's her boss." "No, let's make it complicated. Let's make him a criminal." But my boss is not liking anything. He's starting to make that frown he makes before he's going to go nuclear and... I don't know how, but I finally grow some ovaries and raise my hand and say: "Why does he have to be white? Why can't he be a Latino too?" All the writers are like: "Of course he's got to be white, Loosha you idiot, he's the love interest." All of them bombarding me with reasons why our lead can't possibly have a Latino romantic counterpart – The main one being: "No one will watch."

ABEL. What do they mean "No one will watch"? How the fuck do they know what people will watch.

LUCIA. Well, apparently they do know. Apparently, there are studies and polls that say America won't watch two romantic leads of the same race.

ABEL. Says who?

LUCIA. Says "the research." Because if you have two of the same then it becomes a *black* show, or an *Asian* show, or whatever. But it's not "just" a show anymore. In comedy it's okay, but not in serious stuff. Anyway, for whatever reason…I can't drop it.

ABEL. Good.

LUCIA. Yeah, I won't fucking drop it. I just keep asking, "Why?" They throw out more stupid reasons and I'm still like, "I still don't understand why." Until my boss is like, "Alright. That might not be a bad idea. Pitch it to me tomorrow and we'll see." The room is like…

(She makes a dramatic gasping sound.)

ABEL. Look at you bossing up.

LUCIA. Well, it also might be the thing that finally gets me fired. Who knows. Either way, you know what? You're going to help me.

ABEL. How am I going to help you?

LUCIA. You're going to help me with background stuff. / You're going to make it sound legit. Yes, please-please-por favorcito. I might have overshot the pitch and made it seem like I knew what I was talking about when I said the guy was from the wrong part of the tracks here in LA…

ABEL. What. No thank you.

(Heeell, no!)

ABEL. Which tracks are these exactly? Sorry, no. But good luck with that.

LUCIA. I'm just so tired of those gringos up there making shit sound so fucking cardboard. Have you seen the show? It's basically Taco Bell. / Come on, you'd deny help to a fellow paisana? You really would? I'm invoking the Paisa code.

ABEL. No. Nope.

You're about as close to paisa as I am from having one of those offices upstairs.

LUCIA. You could be a hero right now. It would be so easy for you. And you would save my ass. Seriously, Abel. I need this.

    (Fuuuck. Fine.)

ABEL. You're a brat.

LUCIA. And you're awesome.

ABEL. What do you need to know?

LUCIA. So we know the girl, the detective girl, we know she's independent and that she doesn't need a man. But hopefully-with-my-brilliant-pitch, she's getting one anyway – a Latino one. Now, I pitched that she meets him while she's arresting him / so that it's unexpected and...

ABEL. They fall in love when she arrests him?

LUCIA. Yeah.

ABEL. Not possible. Would never happen.

LUCIA. What wouldn't happen?

ABEL. If she was the arresting officer, then no, she wouldn't fall in love with him.

LUCIA. I disagree with you. People can fall in love in all sorts of situations.

ABEL. This cop thinks this dude committed a crime and she's the arresting officer?

LUCIA. Yeah.

ABEL. And she's the one who makes the actual arrest? Makes him step out of the vehicle, put his hands on the back of his head? When he tries to explain the situation all he gets is his face on the hood of her car, and he has to keep his head down and swallow his fucking pride cuz what's he gonna do? She's the fucking cop bitch with the badge.

And he's just a piece of shit criminal in her eyes.

(Beat.)

No. Never happen.

LUCIA. ...Verga.

(Beat.)

ABEL. But you sayin' this is TV so shit don't gotta make any damn sense.

LUCIA. No, I want it to make sense. I want it to be nuanced and complicated.

ABEL. Well. If the two was to meet somewhere else, somewhere neutral, then maybe it could happen.

LUCIA. Like, before she arrests him? / What, like at a bar or something?

ABEL. Why does she have to arrest him? But yeah, wherever. If she met him and fell for him somewhere and THEN she had to arrest him. I'd like to watch that shit.

(ABEL gets a text. He checks it.)

LUCIA. Yeah. That's like...a little bit more interesting, right? More complicated if they bond and THEN he becomes her foil. Yeah... I'm seeing it.

(Going to her laptop:)

Okay, so if I make it that the guy is from El Sereno – can I say he's from El Sereno? I don't want to do like an East LA kind of stereotype thing...

(ABEL is distracted now.)

ABEL. El Sereno is by East LA. / But yeah, all kinds of
   people live in El Sereno. Good people, bad people.
   Make him from El Sereno.

LUCIA. Oh, it is?
   Awesome. I like the way that sounds anyway. Okay, so
   where do we think they can meet?

ABEL. ...Yeah, I gotta go make a phone call.

LUCIA. "Make a phone call"? No wait. You need to help me
   with this.

      (ABEL, *still looking at his phone:*)

ABEL. Yeah. They can meet at church, how about that?
   / I gotta go call my... I'll see you later if you're still
   around.

      (ABEL *slips out while she types.*)

LUCIA. Oh, that's good. That's actually really good. Okay,
   they meet at church. That can get a whole other aspect
   of her we haven't really seen – which, yes, in a way, the
   whole Catholic thing could be more stereotypically
   Latina, but not if we do it in an unexpected way, right?
   You don't just want her to be this sex-object badass.

      (*Beat.*)

Abel?

      (*Oh, he's gone.*)

Scene Nine

(An episode of the show is on in the background.
LUCIA *watches it from the couch as she eats pizza.*
The vacuum cleaner comes on in the hallway. She
wipes her mouth and presses pause. She opens the
door and peeks out.)

LUCIA. Abel! Abel, ¡ven! Si, ven, plis!

(A moment while **ABEL** *turns off the vacuum*
cleaner and comes over. He enters, looking at his
phone.)

Where have you been?!

ABEL. I couldn't come in yesterday.

LUCIA. Were you sick?

ABEL. No.

LUCIA. ¿Qué pasó entonces?

ABEL. Just stuff.

(Oh. Hmm.)

LUCIA. What's wrong with you?

ABEL. Nothing.

LUCIA. Something's wrong with you. You look all –

ABEL. What did you need?

LUCIA. Abel, he loved it.

ABEL. Who loved it?

LUCIA. My boss loved the pitch we worked on. He loved
it so much that he's letting me write up a whole
background document – which means I get to come up
with the character's entire profile. Now I just have to
show it to him on paper.

ABEL. That's good.

LUCIA. That's not good, that's great. You don't understand.
I haven't done anything right in that room. Not ONE
thing have I gotten right, so I needed something.

ABEL. I'm very glad for you.

LUCIA. Thank you. *(Beat.)* So, I ordered us some pizza and look…

> *(She goes to the mini fridge and opens it Vanna White-style.)*

…got us some beer and we're ready to roll.

ABEL. Who. Us roll?

LUCIA. Yeah. You're my secret weapon. So, let's keep going how we were going: El Sereno; they meet at church. Now, WHAT does he do? Does he have a criminal past? What.

> *(ABEL's just standing there.)*

I bought us pizza. And beer.

ABEL. I can't drink beer at work.

LUCIA. Please, who's gonna know?

ABEL. Famous last words.

LUCIA. Well, then the pizza. It's so good, see? I mean, it's not Chicago-style pizza but it's still pretty good.

> *(ABEL gets distracted by another text.)*

ABEL. I'm not crazy about pizza.

LUCIA. What? That's insane!

ABEL. Hey, tonight we're waxing the second and third floors so I can't really, I just…I don't have a lot of time.

LUCIA. Oh.

ABEL. I mean, I know my job is not as fancy as yours / but I still gotta do it.

LUCIA. Cállate…

I just thought you might want to help me.

> *(ABEL gets a text and texts back. This takes a little while. LUCIA stares at him the whole time.)*

¿Qué onda, Abel?

ABEL. Qué onda "What?" I just can't chit-chat with you. Have to do my job tonight.

LUCIA. Qué gruñón. You in a mood, huh?

ABEL. No, I just got shit going on. Sorry. I'm sorry.

LUCIA. You wanna tell me about it?

ABEL. Not really.

LUCIA. Yeah, you do.

(She closes the door.)

Come on. Sit. Grab a pizza. Yes. You have time for one slice. Ándale, before it gets inedibly cold.

(A beat. He puts the phone in his pocket and sits down.)

ABEL. One day, someone's gonna catch me sitting and it's not you they're gonna fire.

LUCIA. I won't let anyone fire you. Come on. You like mushroom? It's mushroom. The other half is like BBQ chicken.

ABEL. So is it mushroom or is it BBQ chicken?

LUCIA. It's both.

ABEL. You're so not a Mexican, eating pizza.

LUCIA. Best pizza I've ever had was en el DF.

ABEL. In Mexico City? Nah.

LUCIA. Yup. Omaiga. So good.

(ABEL's not too sure, but he takes a slice.)

ABEL. This pizza looks weird.

LUCIA. Yeah, sorry, it's an anorexic LA pizza. That cheese's probably made of negative zero soy product or something.

(He looks at it like "ugh.")

No. Te estoy cotorreando. It's cheese. It's still good.

(ABEL tries that shit:)

ABEL. Okay. It's pretty tasty.

LUCIA. Right?

(Yeah, that shit ain't bad. ABEL eats some more.)

¿Qué tienes?

ABEL. Nothing. I just got some shit going on.

LUCIA. ¿Qué tipo de shit?

ABEL. Just shit.

LUCIA. O sea…qué misterioso.

(They eat for a little bit. She looks at his tattoo.)

What does Semper Fi *[pronounced "fee"]* mean?

ABEL. *(He corrects her pronunciation.)* Semper Fi *["fai"]*.

LUCIA. Is it Latin?

ABEL. Yeah.

LUCIA. Then wouldn't it be "fee" not "fai" if it's Latin?

ABEL. Well, everybody I knew said Semper "Fai."

LUCIA. Everyone you "knew"? What are they, dead?

ABEL. Actually, yeah. Except for two. Although, one might as well have come back dead.

LUCIA. Come back / dead? From where?

ABEL. It's a Marine tattoo. It's the motto. We all got it.

LUCIA. Oh, like the Army. Oh, my God –

ABEL. No, the Marines! / The Marine Corps. Not the Army!

LUCIA. Right. Sorry, I don't…I don't have a lot of exposure with armed forces things. The military. Qué bajón, Abel. I'm sorry, I didn't meant to like make you think of sad things or anything.

ABEL. Doesn't make me sad anymore. It is what it is.

(Shit…)

You know what? Maybe I will take that beer. / Fuck it.

LUCIA. Yeah. You should. Let's, yeah. And then maybe you could help me a teeny tiny bit with my thing?

*(She takes out two beers from the little fridge. She hands one to **ABEL** and closes the blinds – just in case.)*

ABEL. *(Re: artisanal beer.)* Fancy.

LUCIA. This isn't that fancy. It's good though. Love me a good IPA. I'll drink just about any beer you put in front of me. The guy I was…my "ex" or whatever. He hated beer. He was such a wine snob. You know: academic, patronizing – he was THAT guy. He was the kind that smelled his glass of wine and then did this thing...

(She takes a swig of beer and swishes it in her mouth.)

So pretentious. Oh, my God. How did I put up with him?

ABEL. Love is funny like that.

LUCIA. It's so stupid. He kept my dog in the split and I want him back. I want my dog. I have to figure out when to go back and get him. Poor little Captain. He must be missing me so much. I think if I just had a dog here... I think things would be better. God this city makes you feel so lonely, no? I can honestly say I've never been more lonely. Where does one meet people when nobody like walks anywhere here? You're just in your car or you're at work.

ABEL. Don't people make friends at work? I don't know. I don't do the friend thing.

LUCIA. Well, that's a little sad.

ABEL. Why is that sad? That's just real. People always disappoint, man.

LUCIA. Damn.

ABEL. I sound todo bitter, right? Sorry. Okay, what would a normal person say? Hm. *"Why don't you try socializing with your co-workers?"*

LUCIA. Are you kidding? I could never see myself hanging out with any of those miserable douchebags. First of all, they're all white. Not that I have a problem with white people, but they're "that" kind of white, you know what I mean?

ABEL. That's all white people to me.

LUCIA. Right. Plus they're mostly all married and old and rich –

ABEL. Pffftt! **[Loud-ass mouth noise.]**

LUCIA. What?

ABEL. Nothing.

LUCIA. What?

ABEL. No, nada.

LUCIA. Say it.

ABEL. You're rich.

LUCIA. What! Are you kidding? I had to come do this shit because writing short stories for magazines was never going to pay my rent.

> *(He's like, "Whatever you say.")*

ABEL. Please.

LUCIA. I'm being serious.

ABEL. Me too.

LUCIA. Abel, those people upstairs...THEY are fucking rich.

ABEL. Like you.

LUCIA. No, Abel. Real rich. My boss drives a Tesla for God's sake. And that's his second car. That's rich. Not me.

> *(ABEL's still giving her the shady eye.)*

ABEL. Okay.

LUCIA. You're a jerk.

> *(Long pause. Oh, man. That really did offend LUCIA. ABEL pivots back.)*

ABEL. Aw, come on. Did you want me to help you with your thing?

LUCIA. No. Forget it. I'm going to go.

> *(She starts to get her things.)*

ABEL. Come on. Lemme help you. Ask me your questions.

LUCIA. No, I think I'm going to get home. Night.

> *(She leaves ABEL there, feeling real shitty.)*

Scene Ten

(An episode's playing on LUCIA's iMac.)

ROSA. *(Voiceover.)* You better come out, Martínez.

> *(The office is mostly dark except for the flickering light coming from the desktop, which is playing an episode again. Gunshots are heard.)*

MARTÍNEZ. *(Voiceover.)* Martínez? You forgot we grew up together? You've forgotten where you came from, Rosa. You changed.

ROSA. *(Voiceover.)* I'm going to count to three and I swear to God if you don't come out –

> *(Bang, bang, bang. God this show is bad.)*

Scene Eleven

(**ABEL** *enters carrying a six-pack with a bow on it.
He is putting it in the little fridge when he gets a
phone call:*)

ABEL. What's up?

(*Beat.*)

Oh, hey, baby...hi Mamita. What's wrong? What? No.
You're gonna be okay. You're gonna be fine. Bebita,
can you put your Tia Mari on the phone. Yeah, give the
phone to your auntie.

(*Beat.*)

Mari, what the fuck. Why is she freaking out? Well,
why did you give her a bath, then? You know the water
freaks her out. No, you know I can't leave. I can't miss
any more work, Mari.

(*He exits talking.*)

Scene Twelve

(LUCIA's *asleep on the couch when* ABEL *comes in carrying the vacuum cleaner.*)

ABEL. Hey.

Miss Sleeping Beauty.

(*He pokes her. She wakes.*)

LUCIA. What time is it?

ABEL. Two a.m. Man this is late even for you.

LUCIA. Ugh. We have a fucking FaceTime call with John – he's in London – so I'm just waiting it out.

ABEL. Who's John?

LUCIA. My boss.

ABEL. Oh, you on a first-name basis, now? Look at you. Moving on up.

LUCIA. Shut up.

ABEL. "Waiting to talk to *John*."

LUCIA. What am I suppose to call him? Mr. Taylor?

ABEL. No. You call him John.

LUCIA. You're vacuuming tonight?

ABEL. I can do it tomorrow too.

LUCIA. I mean, if you have to do it, do it.

ABEL. I'll do it tomorrow.

LUCIA. Should I have a beer? Yeah, I think I'll have a beer. Do you want one?

ABEL. Um. I do not. Thank you.

(*She goes to grab a beer and then plops back on the couch.*)

LUCIA. You know, I fucking volunteered to stay up for this call. It's actually something we could ask him in an email.

ABEL. Teacher's pet.

LUCIA. I know. So gross. Who the fuck am I? When did I start actually caring about this fucking job? *(Beat.)* Abel, what am I doing with my life?

ABEL. Ah, you gotta call Oprah for the big type questions like that.

LUCIA. You were an *Oprah* fan?

ABEL. That's my girl.

LUCIA. Somehow, I can't see you watching *Oprah*.

ABEL. Oh, yeah. Religiously. That and Maury Povich were the two shows that got me through the roughest six months of my life. Only things we were allowed to watch.

LUCIA. In the Army? Sorry, the military.

ABEL. I don't understand what's so hard about remembering the "Marines"? / No not the Army.

LUCIA. I don't know. Sorry…

ABEL. You need a new liner for the trash.

(ABEL *starts for the door, holding the vacuum cleaner.*)

LUCIA. Hey, what were the roughest six months of your life?

ABEL. Just a bad time in my life.

LUCIA. What happened?

ABEL. Bad shit.

LUCIA. See, I always tell you everything but you never like reciprocate.

ABEL. I got nothing to reciprocate.

LUCIA. I don't know shit about your life.

ABEL. That's not true.

LUCIA. It is. I'm like an open book / and you're like – forget it. Forget it.

ABEL. Yeah, too open sometimes. Like TMI.

LUCIA. It just sucks that you don't trust me yet. But it's fine. No, it's fine.

(Long beat.)

ABEL. The roughest six months of my life were when I was
locked up. When I was incarcerated.

LUCIA. Excuse me?

ABEL. I was in jail.

LUCIA. You were?

ABEL. Yup.

(Pause.)

LUCIA. Don't worry, I'm not going to ask.

ABEL. I don't give a fuck. I'm not embarrassed of why I
ended up in there.

LUCIA. Okay.

ABEL. Your eyes are doing this weird thing.

LUCIA. What weird thing?

ABEL. Where you try to figure out what the hell I could
have done / to get me in –

LUCIA. Not really.

(Long beat. Might as well…)

ABEL. Can I grab one of those after all?

LUCIA. Of course! There's regular beer in there too.

> (**ABEL** *goes to grab a beer from the fridge. He sits
> on the coffee table and drinks for a bit.*)

ABEL. Good stuff.

*(**LUCIA** nods. Then:)*

LUCIA. So why did you, um, how come you went / to –

ABEL. ¿Por qué me metieron al bote?

LUCIA. Ah-ha.

ABEL. Thought you weren't gonna ask.

LUCIA. You're so right. / Sorry.

ABEL. Because I was defending the only woman I'm ever
going to love.

LUCIA. That's so good.

ABEL. What?

LUCIA. That's so good. Sorry, but can I write that down? That's really good.

ABEL. What? For like your character that you're doing?

LUCIA. Yeah.

ABEL. I rather you didn't.

LUCIA. Understood. Sorry.

(She sits back down.)

Alright then. Let's hear this romance novel move.

ABEL. No romance novel move. I was defending my daughter.

LUCIA. Whoa. Your what? / You have a daughter? What is happening right now? Since when did you get a daughter?

ABEL. I said I was defending my daughter. Her mama wanted to take her back to El Salvador and I wasn't... I've always had a daughter.

LUCIA. Since when?

ABEL. Since she was born?

LUCIA. Hold up. Hold up. How long / have I been here and you are only just now...

ABEL. It's not my fault you never asked. Shit.

LUCIA. That's so crazy to me!

ABEL. Why is that so crazy? People have kids. That's not crazy.

LUCIA. I didn't even know you were married. Or with someone or whatever.

ABEL. I'm not.

LUCIA. Okay, this is all... I gotta open a bag of chips here because I'm going to need like sustenance to get all this.

ABEL. You're such an escandalosa.

LUCIA. Corn nuts? / No, guácala, ¿verda?

ABEL. Yeah, no thanks.

LUCIA. Okay, so you're a family man. Or like you have kids.

ABEL. One kid. A six-year-old girl.

LUCIA. And because of her...

ABEL. Right. Cuz of her I was incarcerated.

LUCIA. Okay...?

> (LUCIA *waits for the story.*)

You can't just leave it like that a secas.

ABEL. Well, now I feel all on the spot and shit.

LUCIA. You're the one who offered it up.

ABEL. I know. Why did I do that?

LUCIA. Pregúntale a Oprah – she'd prolly say you want to release it. Okay, so...why were you in the slammer? Oh, God, is that rude to say like that? / I'm just trying to... Oh. Okay. Phew.

ABEL. No, I don't care. I was in the slammer. *(Beat.)* Although, nobody's said "slammer" since Elvis was in *Jail House Rock,* / but sure.

LUCIA. However you say it. The big house..."done time."

ABEL. Okei, but don't...don't use this part on your character guy. They don't know here that I went to prison. I took this job cuz I didn't have to fill that out on the application...and well, I rather they didn't find out. Just in case – knowhatImean?

LUCIA. Oh. Okay. Sure. I won't say anything.

ABEL. Okei.

LUCIA. I'm calling him Joaquin, by the way – the character's name.

ABEL. Oh, I like that name. Strong name.

LUCIA. Thanks. Me too. *(Quick beat.)* Okay, so... Jail time?

> (He "aah's" trying to figure out how to even start this whole thing, then:)

ABEL. Yeah. No, pos my wife, um, ex-wife, she's from El Salvador. She didn't have papers when I met her. But I fell for her hard so then I didn't care about that shit. Nobody thinks that it might be a problem later on down the line. Cuz I was all empelotado so we did everything real fast, the wedding, todo shotgun. And like six months later Melita came. That's my baby girl's name, Melanie, but we call her Melita. But like with all of these situations I'm convinced, it was doomed from the start.

LUCIA. The marriage?

ABEL. Yeah. My ex is real jealous and very passionate. Who knew that Central Americans are so feisty? I always thought they were the calm ones.

LUCIA. Well…they're always having wars and coups down there, so…

ABEL. Yeah, but the women? Aren't they supposed to be all mansitas? That's why I never dealt with a Caribbean or a Columbian, cuz I hear they can be fieras. But I had always heard Central Americans were supposed to be the –

LUCIA. The submissive ones? Well maybe that's what you get for being a macho then.

ABEL. That is true. Joke was on me.

LUCIA. What about Mexican girls? What are they like?

ABEL. Oh, they just trouble.

> (LUCIA *breaks into a smile. Shoot, they both kind of do.*)

Anyway, I didn't know she would turn out to be a liona. She was on her best behavior right up until we moved into our own place in Boyle Heights. Then she turned into a real –

LUCIA. Is that a nice place? I'm still looking to rent something permanent.

ABEL. Ha. You're never going to live in Boyle Heights. You wouldn't last. But it was okay for us and for like around six months everything was good. Pretty nice actually. And then, I don't know what happened but she started – truth be told is I think she was sniffing, but I still can't prove that. She had this aunt that came to live with us and she would always start drama with us. And

the thing is, it was like affecting the baby. She'd leave
with her aunt God-knows-where and I'd come home
and the baby would be all alone, crying in the crib.

LUCIA. That's no good.

ABEL. Yeah. But if I would say anything, the both of them
would pounce on me. Para no hacértela larga we split
up and then it got, just, it got bad. La tia, she came
to my job, not here, I used to be a fireman, actually,
so she came to the firehouse, / y armo un desmadre
saying that "this and that," that now that she had her
citizenship she was going to take the baby back to El
Salvador and not tell me where.

LUCIA. You were a fireman?

ABEL. So I run over there and all her cousins – well, that's
who she says they are, but I never met no cousins of
hers before – there're like six of them in the front yard.
And something didn't look right. The whole thing –
God, I've played it back in my mind, over and over.
Drove me nuts while I was locked up. Something just
wasn't right that day.
   Anyway, I go in and my ex is like half-dressed and all
wyled out. Sweaty and hyper. The baby crying on the
floor there with like two big Salvatrucha-looking dudes.

LUCIA. Like, Mara Salvatrucha? / Like gangbangers?

ABEL. Yeah. But who knows right? They just looked like it
to me. Could have been her cousins but I don't know.

LUCIA. Why were they there?

ABEL. I didn't want to find out. I just wanted my baby. So
I start telling Silvia – that was my ex's name – I tell
her that she can't take my baby. That I won't let her
take her. And let me tell you, hell really hath no fury.
This bitch, she's about this big but she can get crazy.
Throwing shit, spitting out things you wouldn't even
write on a bathroom wall. The Salvatrucha dudes give
us some space I guess because they go outside. And I
grab Melita and try to get her diaper bag to just take
her away while Silvia calms down. But as soon as I do

that, the fucking tia comes out of nowhere and starts beating me with the fucking curling iron and then Silvia just goes nuts and grabs a knife. And she starts waving that thing around.

LUCIA. Jesus Christ…

ABEL. So I'm trying to make my way out the door, but I got the aunt beating me and then Silvia slashing at me. Cutting deep too. And then she stabs me. Like for real. And I say to her, "I got the baby in my arms you fucking maniac! What the fuck is wrong with you?!" No consideration for the baby in my arms. What if she stabbed her? But that bitch won't listen cuz she's like an animal. And when she's about to lunge at me again I just punch her right on the nose.

LUCIA. You actually hit her?

ABEL. Yeah, I just floored her. Blood squirting everywhere.

LUCIA. Oh, my God.

ABEL. Then, the tia comes at me and I roundhouse that fucking bitch too. Nobody's caring about Melita, these fucking bitches. My poor baby in my arms, hysterical. Imagine having to see that? That baby is my whole world. I don't give a fuck if it's her mother, I won't let nobody hurt her.

LUCIA. Qué intenso.

ABEL. I tried walking out but that didn't work so good. I got attacked by all them cousins – me, with my daughter in my arms. Pinches culeros. The cops came and of course, Silvia turned it into me being an abuser and well…

LUCIA. Abel, qué horror.

ABEL. …I'm the one that got locked up.

LUCIA. I'm so sorry, Abel. I'm so sorry.

(LUCIA *puts her hand on* ABEL, *in a comforting way. What else can she say right now?*)

ABEL. Hey, what are you gonna do?

(*Pause.*)

LUCIA. I didn't know you were a fireman.

ABEL. Yup. Engine 57.

LUCIA. I always think that's like the most noble job. That and public school teachers. *(Beat.)* Why did you quit?

ABEL. I didn't quit. You just can't be one anymore if you been to prison.

LUCIA. Oh, Abel.

ABEL. It's fine. I got my daughter with me now, which is all that matters. My mom and my sister help me with her and everything's good.

LUCIA. I'm like...speechless.

> *(Beat.)*

Want another beer?

ABEL. No, I still got –

> *(There's a knock at the door. They freeze.* LUCIA *goes to open it.)*

No no. Wait, can you ask who it is first?

LUCIA. Why?

ABEL. In case it's my boss.

LUCIA. *(Calling offsage.)* Yes? Can I help you?

SUPERVISOR. *(Offstage.)* I'm sorry ma'am. Didn't mean to bother you.

ABEL. That's my supervisor. Fuck, he's looking for me.

LUCIA. Do you need something?

SUPERVISOR. *(Offstage.)* No, that's okay. Thank you.

LUCIA. Alright then!

ABEL. Fuck.

LUCIA. No, it's fine, I can say I called you in here.

ABEL. No. You can't say that – no, please, no te metas. Just let it...please, just.

LUCIA. Okay.

> *(A moment.)*

Qué bajón.

(**ABEL** *is distracted – worried now.*)

LUCIA. Hey, Abel. Don't worry. I won't tell anyone.

(**ABEL** *nods in gratitude.*)

ABEL. Okay, I'm gonna go for it. Ay te watcho.

(**ABEL** *cracks open the door and looks outside. He sneaks out.*)

Scene Thirteen

(ABEL is under the desk, fixing it.)

LUCIA. Ay…what are you doing down there?

ABEL. Fixing your broke-ass desk.

LUCIA. What's wrong with it?

ABEL. The nuts are loose. It happens to these cheap desks –

> *(The phone rings. LUCIA hesitates before answering.)*

LUCIA. *(On the phone.)* Hello? Oh, hi John. *(Beat as he asks the question.)* You mean when he gets set up? *(Beat.)* Yeah, I just think it's like a simple betrayal, like very cut and dry. *(Beat.)* Right. Just the dog hair. You what…? Oh. Um. Oh, my God. Are you sure I'm up for it? *(Beat.)* Okay. If you think I can handle it. Also, is that like legal with the guild? How does stuff like that work? *(Beat.)* Oh, wow. Okay. Yeah, I'll give it a go. You do know I've never written one before. *(Long beat.)* Oh, that's so nice of you to say. Thank you. Yeah, okay. I'll give it a shot and send something up to you. No problem.

> *(She hangs up. She drops the pep, and we see her face has gone bloodless.)*

Holy fuck. Holy fucking shitballs.

ABEL. What the…

LUCIA. Verga, guey.

ABEL. Your mouth.

> *(LUCIA starts walking around in circles, fanning herself with her hands, having your basic freak-out.)*

LUCIA. Shitshitshit…fuck.

ABEL. Alright. I'm not going to ask.

LUCIA. Fuck me, Abel.

ABEL. Excuse me?

LUCIA. Okay…

    Alright…

    I'm either going to need a lot of cocaine to get through this or a fucking protección from a curandera. Straight up magic because… Oh my God!

ABEL. What'd chu do this time?

LUCIA. I hope you know a good Señora.

ABEL. See, right when I start to think you crossed to the gringo side, you remind me that you're true rice and beans. You looking for a bruja now?

LUCIA. Yeah. Who does her spells with the herbs and the candles and shit.

ABEL. That stuff's for widows and fat ladies who've been left by their man.

LUCIA. And for people who just fucked over their work nemesis and might need some protection. Abel, if I don't see you tomorrow, it's because Gary found me in the parking lot and beat the shit out of me.

ABEL. You talking for real? Don't be playing about that shit.

LUCIA. No, but he's for sure going to hate me now. That, I'm one hundred percent certain of. Fuck. But you know what? I'm not going to feel bad.

    Gary is the biggest fucking asshole who's ever walked the Earth. And, on top of that he's a hack. It's on him that his script is a total shitshow. He keeps having to rewrite it and rewrite cuz John keeps giving him notes – and Gary keeps coming back with garbage. Three times now, he comes back to the room with a garbage script. It just keeps getting worse, if that's possible. And today John was…he was mad. / Not like before where he blew his lid. Worse. Cuz he was quiet and seething and just plain scary. And Gary's smarmy jokey-jokes weren't working anymore. So he's up there dying and he pulls this pitch straight from his anus. // He starts pulling stuff out of his ass that makes no fucking sense. Listen to this, he wants to fix this one part where Rosa frames a bad guy, who happens to have allergies by rubbing a dog on a bed. /// A DOG, Abel – on a bed. He's proposing Rosa bring an actual dog to this dirty cop's house and to literally RUB the little animal on a literal bed. *(Beat.)* But what was insane was that all the other writers didn't say shit. They're all "Good Old Boy's Club," letting Gary struggle but not stepping in either. And John is about to lose it. I can tell. Because I recognize that "about to lose it" look. And I don't know how, but I drop straight into my cunt //// and I speak the fuck up: "Wouldn't it be easier to just plant the dog hair? Instead of sneaking in an actual dog?" ///// I'll explain the whole thing. We have to link the dog to this cop-killer. It's stupid. Anyway, John was like, "Finally, ////// someone's using their head." Simple fix. And that was that. But Gary? Oooh. Gary had daggers for me.

ABEL. / What's new. // **[Verbal reaction.]** /// A dog. //// Jesus. Your mouth. ///// Why is she? ////// Hey!

LUCIA. I should have known because everyone leaves and I go into the kitchen for a pinche Diet Coke. Wrong move. I should have come straight down here because that fucker, Gary, corners me in his favorite little harassment nook by the fridge – Abel, can you get up from there please?

(*Oh. Now she notices?*)

ABEL. You so bossy right now.

LUCIA. It's weird with you down there.

(**ABEL** *obliges and comes out from under the desk.*)

ABEL. Ya pues.

LUCIA. So, fucking Gary has me trapped in the kitchen, and he grabs me by the arm.

ABEL. He fucking grabbed you?

LUCIA. Yeah. But, not like that.

ABEL. He put his hands on you, though.

LUCIA. Yeah. He just held me by the elbow like this and came real close –

ABEL. I don't fucking like that.

LUCIA. I know. Thank you for having my back, but it's fine. I'm not scared of him anymore, I can take care of myself.

ABEL. Nobody should put their hands / on you like that.

LUCIA. He was just pissed after that whole rub-a-dog disaster. Anyway, he whispers all gross in my ear, "You know I could have done what you did in there. You can't tell by looking at me and I don't go announcing it to the world, but my grandma was Cuban. So."

ABEL. What does that have to do with – Now I really want to kick his ass.

LUCIA. Exactly! "My grandma was Cuban"? What does that have to do with your bad idea of rubbing a dog on a bed, Gary? My pitch had nothing to do with identity or anything Latino. It was just a good plot pitch. But he was trying to racialize that shit to make me feel this little – to diminish the fact that it was a good idea – but you know what? Fuck him. And fuck him for being on the down low about his Latinoness.

ABEL. Fucking arrepentido. Those are the worst kind. The ones that are ashamed.

LUCIA. What a sellout. He sells his soul every day just so he can have one of those big offices up there. *(Beat.)* What a fucking vendido. *(Beat.)* God, what this place can do to you – it can suck out your soul, sell it to the devil for a good parking spot. Disgusting. Can you believe it? This whole time he's the one who's been giving me the most grief. When he's a Latino.

ABEL. I'm telling you. Crabs in a barrel. That shit holds no loyalty.

LUCIA. It so true. God, I hate him.

ABEL. He'll get his. *(Beat.)* Don't you worry.

LUCIA. Oh, he is getting his. Guess what that phone call was about? I'm going to take a pass at Gary's script. / That means I'm going to get a co-writing credit with

Gary. Which is going to be such a slap in the face when he finds out.

ABEL. Oh, shit.

LUCIA. And right now, just to really fuck with him, I'm planning to do a really good job at it. I'm planning to boss up and write a boss-ass episode, my friend.

ABEL. Yeah, girl. Put your foot in it.

LUCIA. Best revenge after all that shit he put me through. Because unlike him, Abel, I'm an actual writer and can actually write. So fuck Gary. Fuck that arrepentido sellout. This whole TV thing? It's not that fucking hard. It's just making people talk like puppets. It's only television.

ABEL. Right. It's not rocket science.

LUCIA. No, it's not! It's not like writing a novel, is it? A monkey could do it. It's just words.

ABEL. I like what I'm hearing.

LUCIA. Thank you. Alright, let this monkey get to it. She got her a script to write.

ABEL. Alright, changuita.

(She giggles as he starts to go.)

LUCIA. Oh, and if you do have the name of a Señora, I will still take that for hexing purposes. To fuck him up double.

ABEL. Alright, I'll leave you to your broomstick, Sabrina. I want no part / – no, sorry, I want no part of this. Yeah, right. You gettin' that scary look in your eyes, so who knows.

I don't fuck with that brujería shit. Next thing you know, dead people will start appearing all over the place and I ain't about to get a scare when I'm in the mop closet. Fuck that.

LUCIA. Come on, estoy jugando. No creo en esas cosas… Miedoso!

(He's gone. LUCIA takes a deep "in-her-cunt" breath, opens her laptop, and gets the fuck to work.)

Scene Fourteen

(The lights are off. LUCIA *is very still on the floor by the couch.* ABEL *enters and doesn't see her until he's about to leave with the trash can.)*

ABEL. Da hell you doing all in the dark like that?

*(*LUCIA, *barely audible:)*

LUCIA. Nada.

ABEL. ¿Qué tienes?

LUCIA. Nothing.

*(*ABEL *turns on the lights.)*

No, don't. Please.

*(*ABEL *turns them back off and sits on the coffee table.)*

ABEL. You okay?

LUCIA. Yeah.

ABEL. Hm.

(Long beat.)

Are you about to give me some bad news? Did they… did they give you the boot?

LUCIA. Nope.

(Pause.)

ABEL. Your boss yell at you?

LUCIA. Nope. Not at me.

(Silence.)

ABEL. Come on, man. I never seen you quiet before. Me estás worrying.

(More silence.)

Want me to get you something? You got a beer? Maybe you could drink one of your beers.

LUCIA. No, I'm just…no thank you.

ABEL. Okay…

(Pause.)

LUCIA. John fired Gary today.

ABEL. Shit.

LUCIA. I know.

ABEL. Man.

(He goes to sit with her.)

LUCIA. And you know, no matter how you think about it, I had something to do with that.

ABEL. No way. Sorry, but you don't got that much power. Your boss probably noticed that the guy was a pendejo way before you pointed it out.

LUCIA. No. I wish you were right, but no.

ABEL. Did you do something?

LUCIA. I think, in a way, yes. *(Beat.)* The scenes that I've been writing have been good and my boss has been liking that. Which is not good for Gary.

ABEL. Ah, that don't mean it's your fault they fired him. That's on his job performance –

LUCIA. It kinda does. Every time Gary and I turn in the script together, my boss knows who wrote what scene and Gary's scenes are always the problem. So there's been tension the whole week. And this afternoon, John told us we had to come in to work this weekend because we're in such bad shape and…Gary refused. He flat out said, "No." That there was no way we were coming in on his weekend and he got really ugly about it. I think he's just fed up. And…I should have kept my fucking mouth shut…but I blurted out, "John, I can totally come in whenever you need me." *(Beat.)* And I don't have to tell you how Gary reacted.
He started yelling at me and John came to my defense and…well. The whole thing just blew up. *(Pause.)* John asked to speak to Gary alone and the next thing…Gary was clearing out his office.

ABEL. Well, fuck. *(Beat.)* Hey. But you didn't do that. You were just willing to go the extra mile.

LUCIA. I knew how bad Gary would look though. I might have even offered because of that.

ABEL. Fuck him. That's the game, right?

LUCIA. Yeah. That's the game. So does that mean I'm playing it?

ABEL. It's what you've been wanting. To figure out the rules. Well, you're figuring it out.

LUCIA. That guy has a mortgage and kids to feed.

ABEL. I still say you're not all the way responsible. And you showed your boss you're serious and committed and all that. That's a good thing.

LUCIA. Is it? Abel, five months ago, I not only didn't know what I was doing, I didn't give a fuck about this job. I looked down on it so hard. It was all so beneath me. Now, it's become my whole life. It's seriously the only thing I care about. And you don't understand how hard that is to accept. That I've got nothing else.

ABEL. That's not true. Come on. Eye on the prize remember? You're here so you can do that.

(ABEL *points to the book cover.*)

LUCIA. Am I, though? *(Beat.)* If I'm real with myself…do I really have that second book in me? I don't know if I have anything left to say.

(*Beat.*)

ABEL. Listen, I used to get like this when I was locked up. I used to get all in my head. All twisted about shit. But I would make myself crawl out of all that thinking and remind myself to buck up and to do whatever it took to make it through. Because I was seeing guys go crazy in there. And I wasn't going to let myself go nuts. So… If that meant learning to sew patches on uniforms, I sewed patches. Press license plates. Whatever it took to survive in there. You gotta do the same. Whatever it takes to get back to that. To the thing you came here to do. You get me?

(**LUCIA** *nods.*)

Fuck them. You do whatever it takes.

LUCIA. So it's okay?

ABEL. Fuck yeah. You do what it takes. This is called "manning up"! You're going on to that next level shit. You just gotta say to yourself, "Am I willing to do whatever it takes?" Are you?

LUCIA. Apparently, I am.

ABEL. That's my girl.

> (LUCIA *breaks into a smile, cuz* ABEL*'s coach's speech was just so fucking charming. A moment.*)

Shoot. I gotta jet for a bit. We're hanging the Christmas lights tonight so I need to go do that. But do you want me to come back later?

LUCIA. Will you, please?

ABEL. 'Course. I'll bring you some birthday cake from five. They had a birthday and left a bunch.

LUCIA. What kind?

ABEL. Like quadruple chocolate.

LUCIA. Oooh, yes please.

ABEL. Alright. And I'll bring you some milk from the vending machine so you can wash it down.

> (*He starts to go.*)

LUCIA. Hey, Abel.

> (ABEL *turns, but the knot in* LUCIA*'s throat makes it hard to get out the following:*)

I want you to know that this whole time, you're the only person who's been nice to me in this city. The only person who's actually talked to me in any...

> (*She can't finish. It's a bit too much.* ABEL *comes back and sits next to her again.*)

ABEL. Hey, hey...

LUCIA. I just... Thank you. For everything. If you hadn't been so –

ABEL. Come on now.

(He wipes some hair from her face. She lets him. It's a sweet little moment that lingers. Then, abruptly, **LUCIA** *goes in for a kiss. Yup, a straight-up kiss. She jerks back. Oh, fuck. Big mistake.)*

LUCIA. Oh, no.

ABEL. Um…

LUCIA. I fucked everything up. I'm sorry. / *(Beat.)* Just don't get weird with me, okay? Please.

ABEL. Nonono…come on, you're fine.

LUCIA. I don't want us to get weird now. / Can we pretend?

ABEL. We won't.

LUCIA. Oh, God.

ABEL. It's fine.

LUCIA. I'm the worst.

ABEL. No. You're fine. You're just…you're all rattled cuz of the work thing.

LUCIA. I am.

ABEL. Yeah, don't worry about it.

> *(Beat.)*

Rewind. Never happened. *(Beat.)* I'm gonna go do the lights now…

LUCIA. Okay.

ABEL. Night.

> *(He smiles weakly at her before he exits.* **LUCIA** *takes a moment to be like, "What the fuck did I just do?" But then, after a moment of that, something rises in her, and she dusts herself off and dials her office phone.)*

LUCIA. Hey, John. Sorry, are you still here? *(Beat.)* I looked at your notes about Joaquin and I have a pitch. Yeah, I have an idea. Could I come up and – great. Yeah. Okay, I'll be right up.

> *(She hangs up. Alright, this is her bucking up.)*

Scene Fifteen

(ABEL vacuums the office. That's it.)

Scene Sixteen

(The printer is printing when **ABEL** *enters with a fresh trash bag. He starts to dress the bin when the papers start shooting out onto the floor.)*

ABEL. Whoa-whoa whoa.

*(***LUCIA** *enters.)*

LUCIA. Aaah…

(They both go to pick the papers up.)

ABEL. It just started / spitting them out.

LUCIA. I got it, it's okay. I got it. Thank you. You don't have to do that.

*(***ABEL** *keeps helping pick up the papers.)*

ABEL. It's okei. Here you go.

LUCIA. Thanks.

ABEL. Hey, you been a lost girl. You haven't been around much.

LUCIA. I know.

ABEL. You been okay?

LUCIA. What? Oh, yeah. Absolutely. Just been, I've been writing from home while I worked on the episode.

ABEL. Oh, yeah?

LUCIA. Yeah, they let you do that so I took advantage. I was in my PJs all week.

ABEL. Just like in Chicago.

LUCIA. What? Oh, yeah. That's right.

ABEL. You good though?

LUCIA. Oh, yeah. I'm great.

ABEL. Good.

(They stand there for a bit.)

I'm glad.

(They stand there some more.)

Alright, I better get back to it then.

LUCIA. Alright.

> *(He starts to go.)*

Oye, Abel. Could I ask you something?

ABEL. Sure.

LUCIA. How would you feel if I made the, if I used the Marine/Semper Fi thing with Joaquin? The character we were working on?

ABEL. You for real?

LUCIA. Yeah. Like as an homage to you. In your honor type of thing.

ABEL. I don't know. That's okay, I guess.

LUCIA. And I think, to make it positive and complicated and all that – I think he should be a fireman, or like a former fireman. What do you think about that?

ABEL. Yeah, I think that would be good. A Marine and a fireman. I like that.

LUCIA. Oh, good then. Good.

ABEL. When does it show? Like when does it come out on TV.

LUCIA. Well, the script just got approved today, then they have to shoot it. It should air in a few weeks?

ABEL. No shit. It's all happening – like for real. From like a little idea.

LUCIA. I know. From a little idea.

ABEL. So crazy.

LUCIA. I know. My first episode of television. After all that, right?

ABEL. That's right. We have to celebrate at some point.

LUCIA. Yeah, we should.

ABEL. I could go out on my break and get us something. The beer you like.

LUCIA. Oh, that sounds so good.

ABEL. Okay, cool.

LUCIA. Not tonight, though. I've got this thing. Sort of hanging out with someone tonight. So not tonight.

ABEL. Oh, look at you. You made an LA friend.

LUCIA. It's about time, right? Yeah, who knows what this is. Might be nothing, but –

ABEL. Oh. It's like that. Oh, I see.

LUCIA. No, it's like nothing. It's going to be a trainwreck, I should probably cancel.

ABEL. No. Go have a good time.

LUCIA. We'll see. Anyway, next week, I'll stay after and we'll order pizza.

ABEL. Oh, sure. That'll be good.

LUCIA. Alright. I should go. Next week we'll pizza it out, okay?

ABEL. Or whatever, yeah.

LUCIA. Okay, ciao. Bye.

   (He exits.)

Scene Seventeen

(**LUCIA** *is in the middle of watching her episode – hands over her mouth. She's slightly horrified, slightly elated. All we hear is* **ROSA'S LOVE INTEREST** *– who has a pretty distinct voice. Not accent, but voice. The kind that makes you think of a bad guy right away.*)

ROSA'S LOVE INTEREST. *(Voiceover.)* And my ex-wife, that fucking bitch, stabs me in the kidneys while I'm holding my baby girl. So I roundhoused her, knocked her flat on her back, which is where that bitch belonged.

(**ABEL** *comes in without knocking, as always, and* **LUCIA** *quickly shuts the video off.*)

LUCIA. Hey, you! Hi!

ABEL. Hey.

LUCIA. How you been?

ABEL. Pretty good.

LUCIA. Good.

ABEL. You?

LUCIA. Yo super. Todo bien.

ABEL. Glad to hear it.

LUCIA. Haven't seen you in a while.

ABEL. You haven't exactly been down here.

LUCIA. Yeah, my boss let me be in on editing. Editing the episode. So I've been mostly doing that. Who knew that it takes for fucking ever.

ABEL. Yeah, I saw you up there. I kind of tried to wave but I don't think you saw me.

LUCIA. Oh, you did? No, I didn't see you. It makes you semi-blind being in front of the monitors all day.

ABEL. Right. *(Beat.)* How's the thing coming along, then?

LUCIA. The episode?

ABEL. Yeah.

LUCIA. It's okay. It's good. It's done, so. Out of my hands now.

ABEL. When do they show it?

LUCIA. You know, that part I don't know. I've been so focused on finishing it. I'm not sure.

ABEL. I'll look it up.

LUCIA. Yeah.

ABEL. You like how it turned out though?

LUCIA. Yeah, I was just watching it again and I'm kind of proud of it. I'm sure some things could have been better but for a first try, I'm proud of it.

ABEL. You were just watching it in there?

> *(Pointing at the computer.)*

LUCIA. Yeah.

ABEL. Can I see it?

LUCIA. Well, it's so much better on a proper TV. That's the director's cut anyway. You don't want to see that.

ABEL. Ah. Okay. I'll wait. Told my mom and sister about it. We're going to watch it when it comes out.

LUCIA. Great. Awesome. *(Beat.)* My little Captain arrives this weekend and I have to go buy him a crate and a little doggy bed before Petco closes.

ABEL. For real, you getting your dog?

LUCIA. Yeah. Can you believe it? I'm so fucking giddy.

ABEL. I'm glad for you, Lucia.

LUCIA. Thank you. Thanks.

> *(Awkward-ass beat.)*

ABEL. And I hope, I hope you're feeling better about things now.

LUCIA. I am. Sort of. I mean…sort of. Yeah. Bueno. Nos vemos, Abel.

ABEL. Ahi te watcho.

> *(She exits. He goes to take out the trash and then dress the trash can.)*

(He's about to go, but something makes him pivot, which draws him to the iMac where LUCIA *was playing the episode. Does he dare take a look? I mean, he's going to watch it tomorrow, right? It's right there on the desktop, where she left it. He clicks on QuickTime and before he knows it:)*

ROSA'S LOVE INTEREST. *(Voiceover.)* ...Then her mother, that fiera, comes at me with a curling iron so I floor her too. Because I have my daughter, my pobrecita little daughter bleeding and wailing in my arms. Then, all the Salvatruchas attack me and I take out my piece and open up a shower of bullets. / And of course, that's when the cops come but there was no making them understand that I was saving my daughter's life, man. Because, of course I'm the one who got locked up.

> *(*LUCIA *comes back and runs straight to the computer to shut it off.* ABEL *steps away from her – he can't even look at her.)*

LUCIA. What are you doing? Dude, what the fuck are you doing...?

> *(She tries to shut it off but he holds her back, keeps her from the computer. Finally after "locked up," she shuts it off.)*

Why did you do that?

> *(Tense. Tense. Tense.)*

You can't just fucking watch something like that out of context.

ABEL. *(To himself mostly.)* No. I think I got the context.

LUCIA. God, I knew you were not going to know how to watch this.

ABEL. *(Offended by that last piece of condescension.)* Get the fuck out of here.

LUCIA. It's obviously not exactly how you and I worked it. Because it was never going to be. That's not how this works, Abel. This show is a big machine. So many hands go through one of these. So many cooks.

ABEL. Only one cook could have cooked it up like that.

LUCIA. You know what? I'm not going to apologize for this. I asked your permission. You said yes. I put the thing out there. Now, I didn't know my boss was going to cast that guy – he has a certain type of look, but that doesn't mean I think that way about you or the character we came up with. That was something which wasn't in my control. But the thing we're putting out there – the thing *I got to put out there* is complicated and multidimensional. It's a real human being. At least it's my best attempt given the parameters so no, I'm not going to apologize for this.

(ABEL *is looking at* LUCIA *as if he'd been clobbered over the head and he's only just coming to.*)

Hey, I asked you. Didn't I? I asked before I did any of this.

(Beat.)

I asked. And you said yes.

ABEL. I didn't say yes to this shit. You put the prison thing in there – the one thing I asked you not to do.

LUCIA. No, that... I didn't mean for that to get in there. That was sort of a pitch that got out of –

ABEL. You said. From your own fucking mouth, "Okay, I won't put any of that in there." You did. So you're a fucking liar.

LUCIA. Oh, come on. It's a fictional character. Your boss is not going to put two and two together about you having gone to jail. There's no way. I don't think you have to worry about that.

ABEL. And you put Melita in there. You put her in there like nothing.

LUCIA. That's not really her, / Abel...

ABEL. That's my daughter he's talking about like that.

LUCIA. That's not Melita, Abel...

(LUCIA*'s stomped for a bit.*)

Abel, I wanted a real life human up there. I needed him to be real. Not the same old shit we see on Network TV.

ABEL. And you couldn't come up with an idea of your own? You had to take the things someone told you word for word cuz you don't got another way of doing things?

LUCIA. Oh, God. They're not word – Abel, it's not word for word. Please give me a little bit more credit than that.

ABEL. I'm not giving you shit. You just take it anyway. That's how you do.

(*A slap for* LUCIA.)

LUCIA. Abel, he punches a woman. I had to give him something to make him likeable, if not he's just an angry macho punching a woman.

ABEL. Like I was an angry macho punching a woman? / Cuz that's what you been thinking of me this whole time.

LUCIA. No, Abel, that's not at all…
No, / you had your own reason for punching your wife. Please know I understand that. I'm not saying… I'm not saying anything about that. I promise –

ABEL. Oh, man.

LUCIA. I'm just / saying that we had to justify the punching – for the character. Not saying you're a… Oh, God.

ABEL. This whole time. Walking around, judging me.

(*Fuck. Fuck.*)

Oh, man… You had me fooled.

(*Beat.*)

Definitely had that Gary guy fooled.

LUCIA. Don't say that.

ABEL. You know, when I first walked in the door and you were here, sitting there doing your high and mighty thing, I knew you were this. First time I saw you, I knew it. But then I believed you – I believed all the words. Because I'm a fucking idiot. Cuz I shoulda known it; words are you thing, right? That's what a person like you does? Manipulate words for a life? You're real good at that. Man, you're good.

(LUCIA *is stung.*)

LUCIA. *(Weakly.)* I told you I made him a fireman and a vet and...

(ABEL *starts for the door.*)

(Last-ditch effort.) Hey, wait, Abel. You were basically a consultant on this so I hope you'll let me give you part of the script fee I get for this. It's a good chunk of change and I –

ABEL. Fuck you, you're not buying me off with a scrungie, I'm not your fucking maid.

(LUCIA *is gutted. The air punched out of her stomach.*)

(ABEL *gives her one last look of disgust before exiting for good.*)

(LUCIA *stands there, nauseous. She sways there for one dreadful, long moment until she has to lean against the desk...because the breath won't come.*)

Scene Eighteen

(We're in a whole new office. A decked-out office. There's a big flat screen TV mounted on the wall, and the couches are plush and fancy. The desk is a proper desk and the chair, not one of those task chairs. It's a good chair. The whole thing is an upgrade. After a moment, LUCIA enters on the phone. Her clothes are more chic.)

(During the next bit of dialogue she'll grab her things and go off.)

LUCIA. That is what I said to him, John. I told him that. And he still said he couldn't have it done in time for our Monday screening. So I had to do it, because we both know he's been jacking off like this lately and frankly, I'm not putting up with that anymore – so I fired him. Yes, I did. I figured you would have handled it the same way. Yeah, don't worry. Michael can finish the cut. He promised me we would have it to view Monday morning. Yeah, no problem. Of course. That's what I'm here for. Absolutely. See you tomorrow.

(LUCIA has exited.)

(After a long beat, ABEL enters with the vacuum cleaner.)

(He checks the trash; it's empty. It's a moment before he starts vacuuming.)

(Fade to black… to the warped sound of the vacuum cleaner.)